The Mouse and the Wizard

A HINDU FOLKTALE

Retold by Ann Malaspina • Illustrated by Jenny Sylvaine

Published by The Child's World®
1980 Lookout Drive • Mankato, MN 56003-1705
800-599-READ • www.childsworld.com

Acknowledgments
The Child's World®: Mary Berendes, Publishing Director
Red Line Editorial: Editorial direction and production
The Design Lab: Design

ISBN 978-1623236335
LCCN 2013931387

Printed in the United States of America
Mankato, MN
July, 2013
PA02167

n a hut by the mighty river there lived an old wizard who loved to solve problems. With a wave of his magic stick, he could bring rain to a bone-dry field or push back floods during a monsoon.

One day he was having his lunch of rice, flatbread, curries, and yogurt when a mouse peeked out of a hole in the straw mat on the floor. "Come out, little mouse, and I will give you something to eat," the old wizard said.

Wiggling its nose, the mouse sniffed to take in the smell of the wizard's food.

Though he was hungry, the mouse would not leave his hole.

"Come out, little mouse." The wizard dipped his finger in the yogurt and held it out for the mouse.

The mouse's whiskers quivered. "I cannot do that," he said.

"Why not?" asked the old wizard.

"I'm afraid a cat will eat me with its sharp teeth," the mouse said.

"Nonsense," said the old wizard, but he could not convince the timid mouse to leave its hole.

Upon waking from his afternoon nap, the wizard began mixing his potions. The people had brought him many problems that day. A short boy wanted to be tall.

A water buffalo refused to swim in the river. With so much work to do, the old wizard forgot all about the mouse. The wizard spoke the strange words of a spell, and smoke filled the air.

From his hole in the mat, the mouse watched in awe. If the old wizard could help others, perhaps he could solve the mouse's problem, too.

The mouse squeaked softly. "I have a request, old wizard. Please turn me into a cat."

"What did you say?" The old wizard stirred petals in a bowl.

The mouse repeated his request, this time a little louder.

The wizard thought about the mouse's request. "If I turn you into a cat, then you will chase all the mice. Are you certain that will make you happy?"

"Yes, I am certain. I will never be afraid again," said the mouse.

The mouse stood very still, while the old wizard worked up a spell with his magic stick.

"Oh, mouse, be a cat," the wizard said.

A moment later, a cat sat on the straw mat. His teeth were as sharp as any cat's, but he did not chase after mice. The cat crouched by the mouse hole in the mat.

The old wizard put out a bowl of milk. "Come, little cat, and drink some milk," he said.

"I cannot do that," the cat said.

The old wizard raised his eyebrows. "Don't be silly. All cats like to drink milk."

"I'm afraid a dog will eat me with its sharp teeth." The cat's whiskers quivered.

The wizard could not believe his ears. "Now you're scared of a dog?"

The timid cat would not budge from
the mouse hole. Giving up, the wizard
went back to his work.

After a while, the cat said, "Old
wizard, I have a request. Please, turn me
into a dog. I will never be afraid again."

The old wizard had many serious
problems to solve that day. An orange
tree was dropping lemons. A one-horned
rhinoceros had sprouted two horns. But
the cat would not stop bothering him
until he agreed to change him into a dog.

The cat sat very still, while the old wizard raised his magic stick over his cauldron. "Oh, cat, be a dog," he said.

A moment later, a dog sat on the straw mat. His teeth were as sharp as any dog's, but he did not chase after cats. The dog crouched by the mouse hole in the mat.

Stepping outside, the wizard whistled to the dog. "Come, little dog, and play in my garden."

In the wizard's garden, monkeys chattered in the trees and peacocks walked in the shade. A cool breeze blew in from the river. Any dog would be happy to play in such a fine garden.

Instead, the timid dog tried to

squeeze into the mouse hole.

The old wizard reentered the hut and threw up his hands. "What is wrong with you?" he said. "You wanted to be a cat, and I made you into a cat. Then you wanted to be a dog. Now you are a dog, and you are still not happy."

The dog's whiskers quivered. "I'm afraid a fierce tiger will eat me with its sharp teeth."

The old wizard understood the dog's fear. Beyond the garden lay the dark

forest, where tigers roared at night. "Even I am afraid of tigers," he admitted.

The dog was silent, but the wizard guessed what he was thinking.

"I suppose you want to be a tiger," the old wizard said at last.

The dog begged, "Yes, please, old wizard, change me into a tiger. Then I will never be afraid again."

Sighing loudly, the wizard lifted his magic stick. "Oh, dog, be a tiger."

A moment later, a Bengal tiger sat on the straw mat. His teeth were as sharp as any tiger's, but he did not chase after dogs.

The old wizard drew back in fear. What a terrible mistake he had made!

The fierce tiger could swallow him
in one bite. Then the wizard gasped,
shocked at what he saw.

The tiger was trying to squeeze into
the mouse hole! Instead of roaring, the
beast squeaked like a timid mouse. The
wizard called the people of the village to
come see the tiger that was not a tiger.

At first, the villagers were too afraid to enter the wizard's hut. When they heard the tiger squeak and saw him scurry around the hut, they began to laugh. "That's not a tiger. That's a mouse!" they said.

This upset the tiger. He became angry that the wizard allowed people to laugh at him. He thought about trying with all his might to act like a tiger in order to attack the old wizard. But the tiger could not muster up the courage.

The old wizard sensed the tiger's plan. He took pity on the tiger that could not escape the nature of a mouse. The wizard worked up magic to reverse his spells.

"Oh, tiger, be a mouse," he said, waving his magic stick.

A moment later, a tiny mouse scrambled on top of a stool. The mouse wiggled its nose at a fading vision of the tiger it had been. Then it scurried down and disappeared into its hole. The old wizard never saw the mouse again. But sometimes, late at night, he heard something squeak and scurry under his mat. Then he knew that the mouse was finally happy.

India

FOLKTALES

The Bengal tiger is the national animal of India. The tiger lives in the foothills of the Himalayas, a mountain range in northeast India, where the story about the mouse and the wizard takes place.

India holds a great mix of cultures, languages, and religions. Its varied peoples have many colorful folktales of goddesses and weavers, ghosts and tree spirits, elephants and butterflies. The earliest stories of India were shared orally, or by speaking. The stories were later written down and shared with the world.

Many tales reflect the importance of India's religions. One of its major religions is Hinduism. Followers of this religion have produced many great poems and folktales. The story about the mouse and the wizard evolved from retellings based on an ancient Hindu folktale called "The Hermit and the Mouse." This folktale is found in *The Hitopadeśa*, a collection of stories that was first written in Sanskrit many centuries ago. In the original story, the wizard is a hermit who saves a mouse from a crow, and then changes the mouse to a cat, a dog, and finally a tiger. The tiger becomes too full of himself and plans to kill the hermit, so the hermit changes it back to a mouse. The story has since been translated and retold many times.

In the version you just read, the mouse is not happy being himself. He wants to be something else, but when he does, he becomes ungrateful and still cannot change his true nature. Only when he is changed back to his true identity can the mouse be happy. It is a tale that teaches the importance of knowing who you are.

ABOUT THE ILLUSTRATOR

Jenny Sylvaine is French. She was born into a family of artists. An illustrator of children's books, Sylvaine has also worked on video games and on cartoons as a set creator. For the past three years, she has enjoyed drawing and painting in public, alongside storytellers and musicians. Her creativity is influenced by memories of her childhood, when she spent her time looking at everything and dreaming.